We hope you enjoy this book.
Please return or renew it by the due date.
You can renew it at **www.norfolk.gov.uk/libraries**
or by using our free library app. Otherwise you can
phone **0344 800 8020** - please have your library
card and pin ready.
You can sign up for email reminders too.

Withdrawn from Stock
28 OCT 2024

NORFOLK COUNTY COUNCIL
LIBRARY AND INFORMATION SERVICE

OUT OF
MUD

SEAN E AVERY

Warthogs LOVE
to play in mud.

They will slip and slide
and slop about in it…

All.

Day.

Long.

They squash it
between their trotters.

They squelch it through their hair.

They've even
been known...

TO SQUISH IT UP
THEIR NOSTRILS.

That is what **MOST** warthogs love to do at least.

But not Charlie.

"IT'S CHARLESWORTH ACTUALLY. CHARLESWORTH OINKINGTON, AT YOUR SERVICE."

Charlesworth Oinkington was a sophisticated gentleman.

"I THINK YOU'LL FIND THE CORRECT TERM IS GENTLE-HOG, MY DEAR FELLOW."

He was a sophisticated gentle-hog.
Refined and regal as a king; he walked with
his head held high, on his two hind legs.

"ONE CAN'T GO ABOUT ON ALL
FOURS LIKE A COMMON BEAST."

He also enjoyed the finer things in life —
Things like reading poetry, English
Breakfast tea, bird-watching…

"BY GAD! IT'S A
BLUE-FOOTED BOOBY!"

And writing poetry about English
Breakfast tea and bird-watching.

"ROSES ARE RED, VIOLETS ARE BLUE;
AFTER SPOTTING A BOOBY, IT'S TIME FOR A BREW."

Charlesworth was an orderly gentle-hog.

He was clean.

Well-groomed.

"A TUSK SHINED BRIGHT IS A TUSK CLEANED RIGHT."

And he certainly did NOT play in the mud.

No matter how much his friends and
family persuaded him to do so.

"COME IN AND PLAY, CHARLIE!"

"DON'T BE DAFT. I'D NEVER
GET THE STAINS OUT."

Every day, the warthogs would ask Charlesworth to join them in the mud.

"PLEASE CHARLIE?"

His answer was always the same.

"NO."

"PLEASE?"

"NO."

"PLE-"

"NOOOOOOOOOOOOO."

Then, one day...

"MY NAME IS **NOT** CHARLIE! IT'S CHARLESWORTH!"

The gentle-hog roared.

"AND I DO **NOT** NEED HELP FROM A **MUDDY HOG**!"

And with that, Charlesworth stomped off into the bushveld.

Charlesworth was determined
to find new friends.

"NEW SOPHISTICATED
ASSOCIATES."

Sophisticated associates — who were
as clean and orderly as he was.

But, believe it or not, the bushveld was not exactly brimming with creatures who took their personal hygiene quite as seriously as Charlesworth Oinkington did.

"GHASTLY!"

"FOUL!"

"I NEVER THOUGHT I'D SAY THIS, BUT I DO HOPE THAT'S **MUD** THEY'RE THROWING..."

"IT ISN'T."

He was all but ready to give up when he spotted them ...

The flamingos.

How glorious they are! Charlesworth
marvelled to himself.

He made his way across to the flock and
stuck out a trotter to introduce himself.

After a pause, the head flamingo spoke up.

"AND, UM, WHAT EXACTLY IS IT THAT YOU WANT, LITTLE WARTHOG?"

"WHY, I HAVE COME TO JOIN THE FLOCK OF COURSE!"

The flamingos stared at each other in bemusement. They had never seen or heard of anything quite like this before.

"IF YOU'RE TO JOIN OUR FLOCK..."

began the Head Flamingo,

"YOU CAN'T GO ABOUT ON TWO LEGS LIKE A COMMON BEAST."

"OH! BUT I THOUGHT —"

"THE ONLY ACCEPTABLE WAY, IS TO STAND ON A SINGLE LEG AS WE DO."

This made perfect sense to Charlesworth.

It took Charlesworth a little getting used to, but he finally learnt to balance on one leg.

Proud as punch, the young gentle-hog could only imagine how sophisticated he must look.

Charlesworth Oinkington was content. He'd finally found sophisticated associates who were as clean and orderly as he was. There were some problems though. The first was that the flamingos didn't appear to share many of his interests.

They weren't fond of poetry.

They didn't care for English Breakfast tea.

And they REALLY didn't appreciate bird watching.

The flamingos also had a tendency to complain.

"TOO HUMPY!"

"TOO RUMPY!"

"TOO BUMPY!"

They tended
to complain
— A LOT.

"TOO JUMPY."

BOINNG!

Charlesworth found It all quite exhausting.

Then one day, he heard them complaining about his old associates.

"AND WOULD YOU LOOK AT THOSE DISGUSTING WARTHOGS!"

"PLAYING IN MUD?!"

"WALKING ON ALL FOURS?!"

"HOW UNSOPHISTICATED!"

And this was the last straw for the gentle-hog.

Charlesworth decided he'd heard quite enough
from these pompous pink puddle birds.

The flock was flabbergasted.

And Charlesworth Oinkington — the clean, sophisticated gentle-hog —
dropped to all fours and ran to join his friends and family …

In the mud.

Now, if Charlesworth was to be perfectly honest:

He still didn't really enjoy squashing mud between his trotters;
squelching it through his hair; or squishing it up his nostrils —
but he enjoyed being with the muddy hogs that did.

Our Queen Elizabeth

HER EXTRAORDINARY LIFE FROM THE CROWN TO THE CORGIS

KATE WILLIAMS

HELEN SHOESMITH